POBBLE'S HOUSE
POBBLE'S
WAY
OWL'S NEST
DEER'S
BED

Pobble's Way

Written by Simon Van Booy

Illustrated by Wendy Edelson

For my daughter, Madeleine.
May we always skip through the woods
with play in our heads. –SVB

For my husband Gary, my Valentine Bandit.
You've still got my heart,
now and always. –WE

Printed at Keter Press, Israel. First Edition – September 2010
Library of Congress Control Number: 2010920042
ISBN 978-097-9974-66-3

Editor: Shari Dash Greenspan
Graphic Design: The Virtual Paintbrush
This book was typeset in Adobe Jenson Pro.
The illustrations were rendered in layers of transparent watercolor glaze.
Distributed by Independent Publishers Group
Flashlight Press • 527 Empire Blvd. • Brooklyn, NY 11225
www.FlashlightPress.com

Early one evening, after dinner but before bedtime,
Daddy and Pobble crunched through the woods
behind their cottage. Dusk had stilled the creaking trees,
the branches wore long sleeves of snow, and
Pobble's fingers were cozy and warm in a pair of pink mittens.

Daddy smiled and pointed to a floating leaf.

"What is it, Daddy?" Pobble asked.

"It's a butterfly raft!" he said.

Pobble giggled.

"My turn now," Pobble called, pointing
at some chubby winter mushrooms.
"Look at those, Daddy!"

"What are they?" he asked.

"Frog umbrellas!" Pobble announced.

Daddy laughed.

There was so much to see that Pobble wandered off the path and fell into a pile of leaves. When she popped up, Daddy noticed a feather stuck to her hat.

"What's this, Pobble?" he asked.

"Just a tickle stick," Pobble laughed, jiggling the feather under Daddy's chin.

Then they walked hand in hand until Daddy
hoisted Pobble onto his shoulders.
In the excitement, something fell from Pobble's pocket
and landed on the snowy leaves.
It was small and pink and soft as a bunny's chin.

Squirrel crept toward the Something, his nose twitching.
"What is it?" he wondered.
He crept closer and sniffed it.
"Why, it's cotton candy! I'd know that fluffiness anywhere."

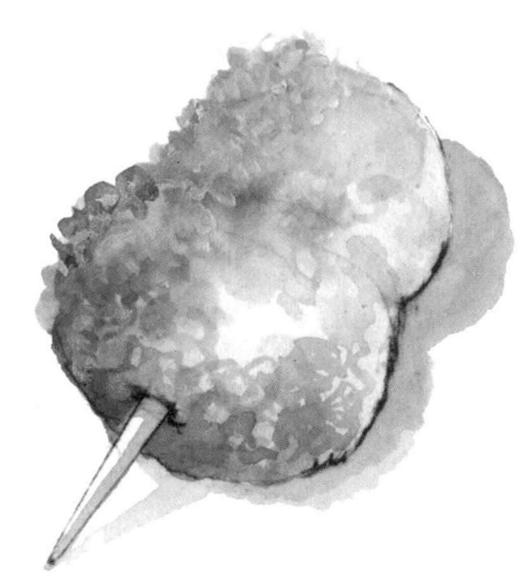

Squirrel popped out his tongue and licked the Something.
"Urgh," he said. "It smells like cotton candy,
but it doesn't taste very sweet."

"That's because it's not cotton candy," squeaked a tiny voice.

"What is it, then?" Squirrel asked.

Mouse scurried over and parked her
plump body on top of the Something.

"Ahhh," she said, burrowing into the soft wool.
"This is an emergency mouse house
for mice who stay out past bedtime
and cannot find their way home in the dark."

"A mouse house?" Squirrel asked. "How interesting.
I suppose you've seen one before?"

"Well, no," Mouse admitted, "but it's definitely a mouse house."

"You're both wrong," Owl declared,
swooping above the Something and landing nearby.
"It's neither cotton candy nor a mouse house."

"Well, what is it, then?" Squirrel asked.

"It's a wing warmer."

"A wing warmer!" Squirrel exclaimed.

"Are you sure?" Mouse squeaked.

"Quite sure," Owl said, lifting it with her claw.
"Imagine how well it would fit a little owlet's wing."

"Well, they are the same shape," Squirrel admitted.

"Of course they are," Owl nodded.
"What you two were arguing about
is nothing more than a wing warmer."

"This is rather odd," Duck interrupted,
strutting over to the Something.
"How did a fish coat get up here?"

"A what?" asked Squirrel, Mouse, and Owl at once.

"A fish coat," repeated Duck.
"When the pond freezes in winter,
fish wear these until spring."

"But Owl said it's a wing warmer," Mouse protested.

"No," Duck assured her. "It is a fish coat.
And it's the most beautiful fish coat
I've seen in all my years on the pond."

"Feel it," Squirrel suggested.
"It's softer than a bunny's chin."

"What's softer than my chin?" Bunny asked.

"This fabulous fish coat," said Squirrel.

"A fish coat!" Bunny giggled,
skipping alongside the Something.
"You're so silly. This is obviously
a carrot carrier."

"But Duck told us it's a fish coat," Mouse whined.

"I suppose it could be worn by a fish," Bunny said,
"but it was really made to carry carrots.
You just slip the carrot in here and go."

"Go?" Duck interrupted. "Go where?"

"Go nibble the carrot," explained Bunny.

Owl shook her head. "I thought bunnies
gobbled carrots the moment they found them."

"Some do, I suppose," Bunny said, looking at her paws.

"Good evening, little ones," Deer said, stepping quietly toward the Something. "What is it? What have you found?"

"Cotton candy," said Squirrel.

"A wing warmer," said Owl.

"A fish coat," said Duck.

"A carrot carrier," said Bunny.

"Well, I still think it's a mouse house," Mouse mumbled.

Deer smiled at her neighbors. "My friends,
don't you know a mitten when you see one?"

"A mitten?" they echoed.

"Never heard of it," Mouse muttered.

"Children wear them on their hands in winter," said Deer.
"And this one belongs to a little girl who is walking
through the woods with her daddy at this very moment."

"Are you sure?" Mouse yawned.

"Yes, I'm sure it's a mitten," Deer said,
"and soon you will see why."

As Daddy's footsteps crunched closer,
the animals slipped away to hide.
The cotton candy, mouse house, wing warmer,
fish coat, carrot carrier, mitten
lay alone and still on the path.

It was almost dark now,
and shadows carpeted the woods.

"What's this, Pobble?" Daddy said,
picking up the lost mitten.

"Oooh, Daddy," Pobble gasped,
"it's a baby cloud!"

Squirrel, Owl, Duck, Bunny, and Deer laughed as Pobble
slipped the baby cloud onto her hand.
Only Mouse didn't laugh. She had fallen asleep.

And as they all went home to their beds,
the Moon came out...

...and pulled her white blanket across the woods.